To my Jack and Riley, and all of our sweet goodnights
—LAS

To Ainhoa,
thanks for always being there
—PS

 little bee books

An imprint of Bonnier Publishing USA
251 Park Avenue South, New York, NY 10010
Text copyright © 2019 by Lisa Ann Scott
Illustrations copyright © 2019 by Paco Sordo
This book is a parody and has not been prepared, approved, or authorized
by the creators of Goodnight Moon or their heirs or representatives.
Manufactured in China   TOP 0119
First Edition
2 4 6 8 10 9 7 5 3 1
Library of Congress Cataloging-in-Publication Data
Names: Scott, Lisa Ann, author. | Sordo, Paco, illustrator.
Title: Goodnight lagoon / by Lisa Ann Scott; pictures by Paco Sordo.
Description: First edition. | New York, NY: Little Bee Books, [2019]
Summary: A young mermaid bids goodnight to all of the objects in her lagoon before falling asleep. |
Identifiers: LCCN 2018030542 | Subjects: | CYAC: Stories in rhyme. | Bedtime—Fiction. |
Mermaids—Fiction. | Marine animals—Fiction. | Classification: LCC PZ8.3.S4276 Goo 2019 |
DDC [E]—dc23 LC record available at https://lccn.loc.gov/2018030542
ISBN 978-1-4998-0845-2
littlebeebooks.com
bonnierpublishingusa.com

GOODNIGHT LAGOON

A *Goodnight Moon* Parody

by Lisa Ann Scott
pictures by Paco Sordo

 little bee books

In the great green lagoon

There was a jellyfish

And a gold doubloon

And a shadow of—

A pirate searching on the dune

And there were three little whales rocking tall sails

And two little seashells
And a pair of ship bells

And an eel in a cave
And a small wave

And a pearl and a fish and a narwhal's first wish

And a clever young mermaid making her tail go *swish*

Goodnight lagoon

Goodnight dune

Goodnight pirate searching on the dune

Goodnight treasure
And the gold doubloon

Goodnight whales
Goodnight sails

Goodnight seashells

And goodnight ship bells

Goodnight ray
And goodnight day

Goodnight eel in cave

And goodnight wave

Goodnight pearl
And goodnight fish

Goodnight octopus

Goodnight wish

And goodnight to the young mermaid whose tail goes *swish*

Goodnight surf

Goodnight deep

Goodnight creatures fast asleep

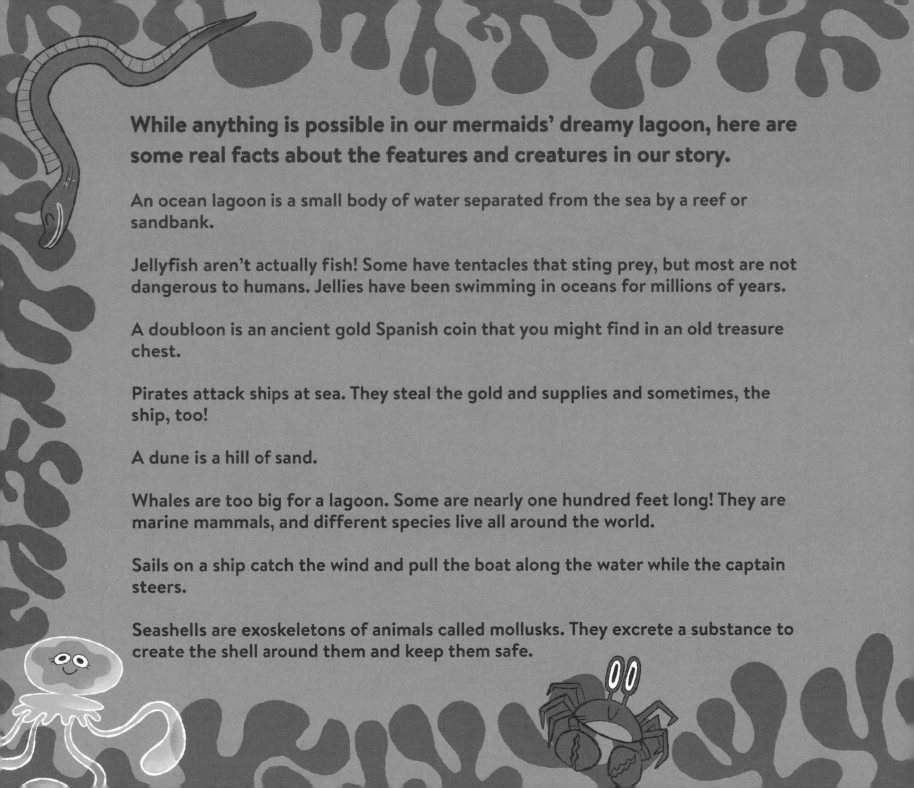

While anything is possible in our mermaids' dreamy lagoon, here are some real facts about the features and creatures in our story.

An ocean lagoon is a small body of water separated from the sea by a reef or sandbank.

Jellyfish aren't actually fish! Some have tentacles that sting prey, but most are not dangerous to humans. Jellies have been swimming in oceans for millions of years.

A doubloon is an ancient gold Spanish coin that you might find in an old treasure chest.

Pirates attack ships at sea. They steal the gold and supplies and sometimes, the ship, too!

A dune is a hill of sand.

Whales are too big for a lagoon. Some are nearly one hundred feet long! They are marine mammals, and different species live all around the world.

Sails on a ship catch the wind and pull the boat along the water while the captain steers.

Seashells are exoskeletons of animals called mollusks. They excrete a substance to create the shell around them and keep them safe.

A ship bell is used to sound the time. Six rings of the bell means it's six o'clock.

An eel might look like a snake, but it's a fish. They hide in caves to surprise their prey.

A pearl forms when an irritant, like a parasite, gets into a mollusk. Mollusks, such as clams and oysters, coat the irritant to protect themselves, which creates a pearl.

There are more than two hundred thousand known species of fish in the world's oceans. Scientists think there are many more that haven't been discovered yet.

Narwhals are a type of whale that live far north in Arctic waters. Their horn is actually a tooth or a tusk! Sometimes they're called the unicorn of the sea.

A mermaid is a mythical creature that is half human, half fish. Mermaids can be found in stories around the world, but they've never been found in real life.

A manta ray is a type of fish. They are gentle and not dangerous to humans.

An octopus is a mollusk with eight arms and a beak. They can shoot out ink in self-defense.